ASTRID LINDGREN

Christmas in the Stable

Illustrated by Harald Wiberg

HODDER & STOUGHTON
LONDON LEICESTER SYDNEY AUCKLAND

A little girl was sitting on her mother's lap, and she asked for a Christmas story. So her mother told her about Christmas in the stable. It was a story of Christmas long ago, in a country far away. But the little girl thought she could see it all happening there at home, in the stable out in the farmyard.

This is the story her mother told:

One evening long ago a man and a woman came along the road at dusk. They had walked a long way, so they were tired and they wanted to go to sleep. But they did not know where they could rest. The lights were out in all the farmhouses. People were already asleep in the houses, and no one cared about the travellers who were still on the road. It was dark and cold that evening long ago. There were no stars shining in the sky.

Then the travellers came to a stable by the roadside. The man opened the door and shone his lantern inside. He wanted to see if there were any animals there. Places where animals sleep are warm, and the two travellers were cold and tired.

Yes, there were some animals in the stable. They were already asleep, but they woke up when they heard the door creak and saw the travellers come in. They saw the woman standing there in the light of the lantern, but they did not know why she had come to their stable so late in the evening.

But perhaps they could feel that the woman was cold and tired and hungry. Perhaps the horse felt it, when she thrust her fingers into his mane to warm them.

Perhaps the cow felt it when the woman milked her and drank the good warm milk.

Perhaps the sheep felt it too. When the woman lay down to sleep in the straw they crowded round her to keep her warm.

Then night fell over the stable and
the man and woman and animals inside.
But at the darkest time of night the first cry of a
new-born baby broke the silence. At the same
moment all the stars shone out in the sky. One star
was bigger and brighter than all the rest. It stood
right over the stable shining clear and bright.

There were shepherds out in the fields that night. They had gone to fetch home some sheep which were still grazing in the open, although it was already winter-time. The shepherds saw the star over the stable. They saw the whole sky blazing with light.

'Why is that star shining over our stable?' the shepherds asked each other. 'Let us go and see what has happened.' They hurried home with their sheep and lambs along the snow-covered paths.

They found a new-born baby in the stable. He was lying in his mother's arms. 'That star is shining for the baby,' said the shepherds. 'We never had a baby born in our stable before.'

The baby wanted to go to sleep, but there was no cradle or bed for him in the stable. There was only a manger. The mother put her baby to bed in the manger. The horse stood quietly beside it and watched her. Perhaps he could see that the baby wanted his manger for a cradle.

So the night passed by. The baby was asleep. The animals and the shepherds stood round the manger in silence. Everything was quiet.

The Christmas star shone over the old stable. For it was Christmas when this happened, Christmas long ago. The first Christmas of all.

ISBN 0 340 03266 9

Copyright © 1961 Astrid Lindgren and Harald Wiberg
This translation copyright © 1963 Hodder & Stoughton Ltd.
First published in Sweden in 1961 under the title of Jul i Stallet.
This edition first published in 1963 by Brockhampton Press Ltd
(now Hodder & Stoughton Children's Books), Salisbury Road, Leicester.

Sixth impression 1975

Printed in Great Britain by Ebenezer Baylis & Son Ltd, Leicester and London